TBH, IDK What's Next

Also by Lisa Greenwald

TBH, IDK What's Next

KATHERINE TEGEN BOOKS
An Imprint of HarperCollins Publishers

BY LISA GREENWALD
Author of *11 Before 12*

Katherine Tegen Books is an imprint of HarperCollins Publishers.

TBH, IDK What's Next

www.harpercollinschildrens.com
ISBN 978-0-06-268999-3
Typography by Aurora Parlagreco
19 20 21 22 23 SCP 10 9 8 7 6 5 4 3 2 1
❖
First Edition

For Sonia, who's been my friend since we were CPG4eva's age!

Prianka, Vishal

OMG I am sneaking 2 use the phone

Don't like being so disconnected

Don't like camping either

R u there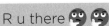

VISHAL

Yes hi

PRIANKA

That's all u can say?

I am breaking rules here

VISHAL

Sorry

1

Grrrrrr I gtg just got cau

From: Outdoor Explorers Staff
To: Mr. And Mrs. Basak
Subject: Screen policy

Dear Mr. And Mrs. Basak,

Prianka was caught using her phone earlier today to text a friend. As you know, we are completely screen-free on Outdoor Explorers. The counselors have confiscated her phone and will return it at the end of the trip.

She has received a warning. Any further infractions will require us to take more serious action.

With best wishes,
The Outdoor Explorers Staff

Guysssss, can you believe after all that buildup we only have a few days left of our camping trip? OMG. I was totally dreading this and I loved it beyond belief. It went so fast. I am so sad it's over. Although it will be good to get away from Darren's 24/7 guitar playing! xoxo Gabby

I know! I feel like it was one of those life-changing experiences where we look back and are so amazed it even happened. I mean, for the rest of our lives we are going to remember waking up at 5 a.m. and going on that crazy long hike and watching the sunrise. I really want to do it again next summer. Maybe even the longer one. Gabby, you're like a different person when living in a tent. You're like so hyper and friendly and silly all the time. I love it! Bring this Gabby back to school with us! :) Love u guys forever, Cece

You guys! OMG. You are all crying about this trip ending and I am soooo excited to get home. SO happy I only got in trouble one time. And hahaha they have no idea how many times I snuck my phone. Who knew I was such a rebel? I guess camping brings out something different in each of us—and not all good things!

Is there something wrong with me that I hate hiking and really don't like being outside that much? I am nervous that I am more of an indoor person. What does this mean for my future life? Netflix, I miss you!!!!!

But for real—since I was SO not into this camping thing, can we please make a pact that when we get home we make it the best summer ever (for the time I'm around which isn't much bc of India). Okay? Promise? Respond below.

Xoxoxoxoxo PRI THE EXTRAORDINARY

Lol, Pri! You like being outside, though. You love the beach and that's nature too. Duh. I am amazed we kept this notebook going the whole time and no one stole it. Or tried to snoop. Do you think we'll keep in touch with Ivy? I like her a lot but I don't know. Is it rude that we talked about her here? Do you think this notebook is the same as group chat?

Ack. What if she does try to snoop? She's just so amazing, though, right?

Yes to the pact. When we get home it will be Best Summer Ever 2.0!!!

Yes to the pact. Of course.

And am I really that different here? I don't know.
But thanks for the compliment!

But also, Pri, not everyone likes the same things.
Duh. That's why there's chocolate and vanilla (thanks
to my grandma for teaching me that expression).

Yes to the Ivy thing. She is SO cool. She taught us
how to change under our towels. Hello, life skill! We
have to keep in touch with her. I am just so glad
we had so many cool bunkmates. How will I go
back to just living with my mom at home? Boo hoo.
Luv, Gabs

I didn't expect to be homesick! I don't even like
my parents that much. JK. I love them, but
for real. I leave for India pretty soon after we
get home. Then I'll be homesick for you two!

WAHHHH.

Anyway, Operation Best Summer Ever 2.0 starts in a few days! Xo Pri

Mom, Prianka

MOM

Prianka darling, I hope you do not see this message, since you are not supposed to be on your phone. But if you do, we are sorry you do not like camping. But that is not an excuse to break the rules. We will discuss more when you return home. We love you. Mama and Papa

From: Yorkville Middle School Administrators
To: Yorkville Middle School Students
Subject: Summer assignment

Hello, Students!

Hope you're enjoying summer. Don't forget to work on this summer's writing assignment: **How have you changed since this time last year?**

With permission, some of the essays will be posted (without names).

All the best,
Yorkville Middle School administrators & staff

OMG, Pri. I can't believe you snatched your phone back. But pls stop showing us. I don't want to know about school right now. Feels so far away and I like that. Will deal with assignment when home.
Xo Gabs

Same. Love, Cece

OUTDOOR EXPLORERS ROSTER

Dear Explorers,

Well, our camping trip is sadly coming to an end. Together we learned so much—how to work together, how to live together, how to enjoy our beautiful planet Earth together. We learned how to be 100% screen-free!

And now we will return home. We will share all that we have learned and experienced with our friends and families.

Together we can heal the world. (Yeah! Yeah!)

Please find a roster of all the participants and please keep in touch with everyone—including your counselors!

We'll be sharing our online photo album with all of you as soon as we get home and return to our screens. You will be able to update and add to it, so we can all stay up-to-date on each other's lives.

We miss you already!
Your fabulous counselors—

DARREN, **Aviva,** George, Marley, Everett, and Vee

I am back to poetry
That's how sad I am on this trip
Cece and Gabs love it
I do not
They are happy outdoors
I am not
I am alone with my feelings
So alone
I am not meant for camping
And I was so excited to do this trip
Life is odd

Dear Cece,

Camp is super fun. Soon we are going to find out who the captains are for the Olympics. I am praying they pick me. I've been trying to be a good "leader." That's what they look for. How's camping? Hope you're having fun. I'm thinking about trying out for the swim team this year. What do you think?

Miss you.

Luv, Mara ♡ xoxo

Cecily Anderson

Outdoor Explorers

P.O. Box 307

Eagle Creek, MA 01221

Um, Cece, do we really have to write a note to each person on the trip? Wahhh. I know you will love it but I am wahhh. So this is your note. LOL. Xoxo ILYSM, Pri

Gabs, you're the best. Thanks for sitting with me all those nights when I was homesick. I still think the cheese here tastes like toothpaste. LOL. Potty pals 4ever. Will miss u when I have to pee alone at home. ILY4evs, P

Hi, Jake—it was fun getting to know you this summer. Good luck with your science fair thing. —Prianka

Dear Cecily, I hope you can read my handwriting. It's really bad. HAHAHA. Anyway, it was so fun getting to know you. I can't believe you were able to dive from that high boulder into the waterfall. WOW. Hope you'll keep in touch. —Jaylen

Hi, Gabby, never forget slimy rocks and heaps of potatoes. LOL. You're so funny. You're also the most fun, daring, adventurous, chill girl I've ever met. Can I please come sleep over? I know everyone loves you, but can I be your BFFFFFFFFFF? Say yes. I LOVE YOU! xoxo Ivy

Dear Prianka,

What can I say? I know this trip was a struggle but you powered through and our group was better because you were here. Aren't you glad you didn't go home early? I hope you will always stay the bold, confident, powerhouse girl that you are. It's okay to say what's on your mind and I am glad you know that. The world needs strong superhero girls like Prianka Basak! Please keep in touch. Lots of love, Vee

Ummm guys I'm tucking this note into shared notebook because I don't want anyone on this bus to see it and I am scared I will drop it. Read asap and tell me what you think. OMG.

Dear Gabby,

Well, we were supposed to write a note to every person and I did but I saved the last one for you and it took me so long to figure out what to write so that's why you are getting it so late. The whole time we've been on this trip I wanted to talk to you and get to know you better but I was so shy. I will never forget the night we had to do clean up together. You were so funny the way you were trying to sweep the eating area. Anyway, I think you're really awesome. It would be great if we could keep in touch. I know it's weird because we didn't talk a ton on the trip. But maybe we can get to know each other better now. My cousins live kinda near you. I hope you don't think I am totally crazy. I just think you're really fun and smart and super pretty. Also, I don't usually write these notes to girls. Just in case you were wondering.

Okay, bye.

—Eli

HOME HOME HOME HOME HOME

(P) (C) (G)

PRIANKA

Guysssss, reunited w my 📱📱📱 & it feels soooooooo goooooooodddddddd 👏👏👏👏

Where r u 👁•• 👁••

R u serious?! U r not so excited 2 be back with ur 📱📱📱?!??!?

I don't believe this 🙄 🙄 🙄

& hello - we r supposed 2 b starting BEST SUMMER EVA 2.0 rn 👏👏👏

Where r u ⁉️⁉️⁉️⁉️⁉️

20

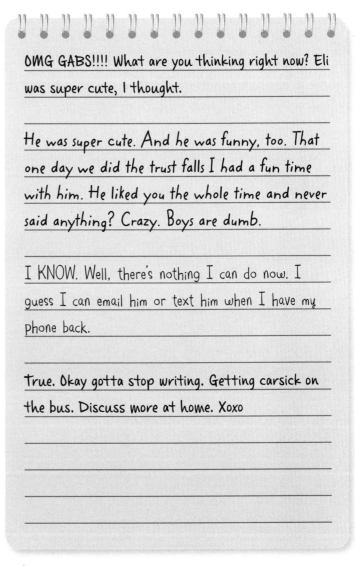

OMG GABS!!!! What are you thinking right now? Eli was super cute, I thought.

He was super cute. And he was funny, too. That one day we did the trust falls I had a fun time with him. He liked you the whole time and never said anything? Crazy. Boys are dumb.

I KNOW. Well, there's nothing I can do now. I guess I can email him or text him when I have my phone back.

True. Okay gotta stop writing. Getting carsick on the bus. Discuss more at home. Xoxo

17

Wait, Gabs, I am writing you on the back of this sheet because I can't find paper and also don't want to use notebook if Cece isn't writing now. BUT what do you think? Is Eli on this bus?

No, his parents picked him up because they're going to Vermont on vacay. I only know that because they drive like a gigantic SUV, which is weird bc we were on a nature trip. Whatever though. Crazy about the note, right?

YES! And funny we are writing this on a paper about s'mores. Way to waste paper, people! Cracks me up. Are you going to contact him?

Well, s'mores are important. And as for Eli... I don't know! Maybe?

Okay out of room on this paper. Going to dig in my backpack for something else.

HOW TO MAKE THE PERFECT S'MORE
By George and Marley

1. Make sure your graham crackers are ready and out of the package.

2. Make sure your chocolate is broken into small pieces.

3. Put chocolate on each half of graham cracker.

4. Find the perfect roasting stick.

5. Gently insert stick into marshmallow.

6. Stand close to fire but not directly on top of fire.

7. Roast marshmallow until one side is charred but do not let the entire marshmallow get charred.

8. Gently take marshmallow off stick.

9. Place the charred side onto the chocolate piece.

10. Put both halves of graham crackers together with marshmallow and chocolate oozing together in the middle.

11. VOILÀ! THE PERFECT S'MORE!

Hey, Gabs, i know you're
camping and won't see this for
a while but check out what i
made at art camp. We had to
take a photo and then paint it
and i had a photo of you from
that locker clean-out day. You
can keep this.

Peace, Colin

HOME HOME HOME HOME HOME

P C G

GABRIELLE

Sorry missed these texts 😳😭🙀

Guess what??? Colin dropped off a drawing @ my house when I was away

Omg 🙀🙀🙀

PRIANKA

Gabs, u have 2 boys in love with you 🙄💔🖤

GABRIELLE

Haha no 🙀🙀🙀

Anyway I don't like either I don't think

PRIANKA

Colin's such a talented artist

Why did I have no idea

GABRIELLE

IDK he really is though

His art stuff makes him so much cuter I think 😌 😊

PRIANKA

4 real

GABRIELLE

Haha yeah artists are amazing

PRIANKA

Haha ok

CECILY

Hi, guys, I am so behind on these texts
😨 😰 😲 😦

Was looking @ website 4 camping trip next summer LOL

Of course u were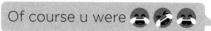

What? I loved it 😍😍😍😍😍

I know 😐😑😣🙄

I did too 😎😎

Don't hate, Pri 🙄🙄

U know I was sooooooo scared 2 go
😨😮😳🤭🤭

I am not hating

Gabs, u were so 😬😫 2 go & ended up
loving it soooo much 🤭🤭

It's ok 4 us to like diff things

PRIANKA

But omg that was so not my thing

CECILY

WE KNOW

PRIANKA

Don't scream @ me

CECILY

Sorry

It was just super obv u weren't into it 😠😠😠😠

I felt really bad the whole time 😫😫

PRIANKA

It didn't stop u from having fun

Right? 🤸🤸🤸🤸

25

GABRIELLE

No

PRIANKA

Cece **??**

CECILY

No but I did feel bad

PRIANKA

Well sorry

CECILY

It's ok

I gtg

Trying to still stay kinda screen-free

PRIANKA

U too, Gabs?

GABRIELLE

IDK we'll see

PRIANKA

Guysssssss

Who has started school essay thingy

CECILY

We just got home but I've been writing it in my mind

LOL I've written a bit 😹 😹 😝 😝

Doesn't need to be that long 📕 📕 📕

PRIANKA

K going 2 catch up on 📺 📺 📺 📺 📺

GABRIELLE

K smooches 💋 😘 😽

Double smooches 😽 😽 😽 😽

PRIANKA

Ily2sm 💘 🤍 💘 💞 🤍

27

Prianka Basak

Summer essay assignment

The concept of change is very strange. (I didn't mean for that to rhyme, sorry.) It's because we don't see ourselves changing. It just sort of happens. But the thing is, I think I've changed a lot since last summer. I used to go along with whatever people wanted, and now I speak up. I'm okay with saying what things I like and what things I don't like. I'm proud to be more outspoken and open with my feelings.

Gabrielle, Colin

GABRIELLE

Hi 👋🏻👋🏾👋🏻👋🏾

COLIN

You're home?

GABRIELLE

Yup 👍🏻👍🏾

I got ur painting 🎨🖼️🖌️👨🎨

Thank u 👏🏻👏🏾👏🏻

COLIN

Do u like it

GABRIELLE

Yeah it's really good

COLIN

Thanx

GABRIELLE

What r u working on now 🖌️ 🧑‍🦰 🎨

COLIN

Different stuff IDK

GABRIELLE

Take pics & send 2 me 🖼️ 🖼️

COLIN

Maybe but they r not done yet

GABRIELLE

Ok 👌

COLIN

Will u be @ the pool this week

GABRIELLE

Prob yeah 🌊 🗑️ 🗑️

But I go on vacay with my dad soon 🌅 🌅 👜 🎒

COLIN

Cool

GABRIELLE

IDK I am kinda nervous 2 go

COLIN

y?

GABRIELLE

Just am

COLIN

Ok

I bet it'll be fun

See ya

From: Outdoor Explorers Staff
To: Outdoor Explorers Group
Subject: Hello!

Hello, Outdoor Explorers!

By now you're settling into life at home. We miss you! At the bottom of this email you'll find a link to our online photo album. You can like photos, comment on photos, download them, share them with friends, etc. You can add photos, too, to keep everyone up-to-date on your lives! There's also an option to make a memory book. We hope this will help you remember the amazing time we all had together on our Outdoor Explorers experience.

Stay in touch!
George (and all of your other counselors)

"Wherever you go . . . go with all your heart."—Confucius

Click here!

THESE PHOTOS

PRIANKA

Guyysssss, these photos are really good

I look like I am having the best time ever 😌😂🤣

GABRIELLE

Haha maybe u had more fun than u think 😛😝😜

CECILY

Yeah! 👏👏

If an online album shows you having fun, maybe that's all u need to know that you had fun 😜🤭

PRIANKA

Ummm ⁉️⁉️⁉️⁉️

CECILY

Gabs, did u see how many peeps hearted the one of u on the tire swing ❤️❤️❤️❤️

PRIANKA

I didn't see u could ❤️ the pics

GABRIELLE

Oh just checked 😻😻😻😻😻😻😻😻

Wowie ❣️❣️❣️❣️

I'm popular 😻😻

This album is the coolest ❣️

We can add our own pics too 🎉🎊🎉

PRIANKA

Could be Eli doing every heart LOL 🙄🙄🙄🙄

CECILY

LOL, Gabs, u r popular 👍👍👍

GABRIELLE

Haha thanx 🐱🐱

4 real tho - I really miss the group 😥😥

I didn't realize how amazing it was 2 be w/ so many peeps all @ the same time 👫 👫

Feels like such a letdown 2 be home now 😾😾😾😾

CECILY

Oh, Gabs 😿😿😿

But we r here w/ u 🐰 🐰 🐰

GABRIELLE

Not really w/ me but yeah 😼😼😼

PRIANKA

& what about Best Summer Ever 2.0?

35

Let's get started on that peeps, & have fun

GABRIELLE

LOL yeah but not the same

PRIANKA

Well let's try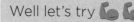

GABRIELLE

K

R U GUYS HOME

VICTORIA

Friendsssssss, I think ur 🏠 by now

LMK

VICTORIA

Creative writing camp in Philly was sooooooo fab 🖋️🖋️🖋️🖋️📖📖📖

PRIANKA

Yesssss we r finally home 🏡🏡🏡🏡🏡

Thanx to the all powerful Durga

VICTORIA

?

PRIANKA

Nvm hindu goddess

VICTORIA

Oh ok 😍🥴

So how was it **?????**

PRIANKA

Ummmm I didn't love 🐺🐺

But based on this online photo album they sent I look like I am having the time of my life 😂🤣😂🤣😆

VICTORIA

LOL, Pri

PRIANKA

IDK it was ok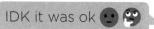

I prefer real beds and nice showers

Does that mean I'm super fancy

VICTORIA

No I don't think so 👍 👍

PRIANKA

Anyway now we r home and it will be Best Summer Ever 2.0 🖤 🖤 🖤 🖤 🖤

w/ u Vic!!!!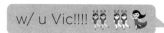

VICTORIA

Yay! 🎊 🎉 💞

Where r Cece and Gabs ❓❓

PRIANKA

IDK

Still trying 2 b screen-free I think

VICTORIA

OMG 4 real?

PRIANKA

I think so

VICTORIA

R u going 2 the pool 2morrow

PRIANKA

Yeah def

Need 2 get it all in b4 we leave 4 India

VICTORIA

K text me when u r on the way & I'll meet u

PRIANKA

K cool

VICTORIA

Same goes 4 u, Gabs and Cece, if they ever see this LOL 😂 🤣 😂 🤣

PRIANKA

LOL LOL LOL 😂 😂 😂 😂 😂 😂 😂 😂

Dear Journal,

Well, I'm home from the camping trip. I'm sorry I didn't bring you with me because there were lots of times when I wanted to write in you. But the thing is, I was scared you'd get lost and someone would read you and everyone would know my most private thoughts. So it was safer to leave you at home. I'm pretty sure Ingrid doesn't really care that much about my personal life to read you behind my back, but I could be wrong. It's usually the little sister who tries to snoop, not the big. Who knows.

Anyway, I had so much fun on the camping trip. Gabs had fun, too. Pri not so much. She was all gung ho until like the second we got there and then she was kind of miserable. She didn't want to do any of the activities. She wasn't super into meeting new friends either. Like, Gabby and I became good friends with this girl Ivy and with this group of three girls from

Toronto, Canada. But Pri just hung with us and didn't seem super friendly. I don't know what happened to her. I didn't let it totally ruin my time but it did affect me. I kept feeling bad for her and trying as hard as I could to get her to have fun.

I thought about Mara pretty much every day. I wondered what she was doing at camp and if she was having fun. We wrote a few letters but that was it. But next few weeks Gabs and Pri will be away and I think Mara will be coming home from camp soon so hopefully we can hang out a lot before school starts. I wonder if her feelings will ever change.

I am so sleepy. Gotta go.

Love, Cecily

Summer Essay by Prianka Basak – draft 2

I originally wrote this essay by hand but I bet it will be more professional if I type it. I don't know why I wrote that. I will probably delete this paragraph.

Change is one of the biggest factors in our lives—we are always changing. We have no control over it. I can't say that I like change but I also can't say that I hate it.

One way that I've changed is that I now accept the fact that changes are coming. Also, that we don't like everything we think we will like. And it's okay to be open and speak our minds. We don't have to like the same things as our friends.

Also there is always room for change. For example, I didn't have fun on my first summer trip but I am making changes now so that the rest of my summer is fab.

Heyyyyyy

JAKE

Yooooooo camping peeps

I started the biggest group text in the history of the world

Haha IDK but u r all on here

IVY

Hiiiiii

I miss u guys sooooo much 😫😫😫😫😫😫

DIMAH

OMG same same same 😿😿😿

CLARA

Hiiiii, everyone 🎈🎈🎈

CLARA

How's life @ home

JAYLEN

Hey, guys

DIMAH

Ivy, what is my life without you???

I need u telling me what 2 wear

IVY

Same, girl

I can't go to sleep without ur amazing bedtime stories

DIMAH

OMG

JAKE

So lost already in this chat

Unknown, Gabrielle

MAYBE: IVY

Gabs?

GABRIELLE

Hiiiiiii

MAYBE: IVY

Do u know who this is ⁇

GABRIELLE

Yesssss my phone says maybe Ivy lol

MAYBE: IVY

LOL LOL so add me so it knows 🧜‍♀️🧜‍♀️

GABRIELLE

K done

IVY

How r u 😎😎

IVY

I miss u soooooo much 😭😭

GABRIELLE

Same 🐺🐺🐺

Wish we were still on the trip ⛺🌳🌲🏔️

I really miss being all together and having people around all the time 💔💔💔

Now its just me & my mom & it's quiet and boring 👧👩

IVY

What about Pri and Cece 👯👯

GABRIELLE

They're here but not like w/ me 24/7 like we all were ya know 🐺😭🐺😭

IVY

Yeah I miss the trip so much 2 🐺🐺🐺🐺

But I have fun summer stuff coming up ☀️😎🌞🍉🍦🍧🏖️⛱️🌅🕶️

47

GABRIELLE

Cool

What stuff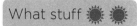

IVY

A trip with my whole fam to this awesome resort in Maine with waterskiing & my mom & I are gonna try and see 1 Broadway show a week & back 2 school shopping spree so yayyyyy 👏👏👏

What about u ☀️ ☀️

GABRIELLE

Just hanging @ the pool with Pri & Cece 👧👧👧👧👧

Trip with my dad soon 👨👨👨

He does not have mustache lol 🐺🐺🐺

IVY

Oooooohhhhh where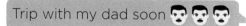

48

GABRIELLE

Austin Texas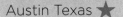

IVY

So cool

GABRIELLE

IDK

We r going with his friend and friend's kids so IDK

I don't really know them at all & it's with 2 dad BFFs so IDK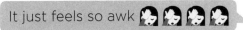

It just feels so awk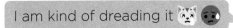

I am kind of dreading it

IVY

I bet it'll be cool

I gtg tho

Love u

GABRIELLE

Bye xoxox

49

Gabrielle, Cecily

G   C

GABRIELLE

Have u noticed how Ivy's life is like so perfect 💯 🙌 🤞

CECILY

Wdym 👻

GABRIELLE

All the pics she posts 🕺 🕺

Her fancy backyard with the pool and firepit and stuff 🔥 🌲 🌳 🌊

CECILY

Oh um

GABRIELLE

U didn't notice ❓‼️

CECILY

Not really

I wonder if Pri noticed

CECILY

Why isn't she on this text ?

GABRIELLE

IDK she was so anti the trip so

Does Ivy text u ??

CECILY

No just the group chats but her dog is super cute

GABRIELLE

Ha even her dog is perfect 💯 🙌 🐶

She has 2 pink ribbons 🎀 💝

CECILY

Haha IDK

U notice all this stuff ?!?

U don't

CECILY

No

GABRIELLE

I feel like my life is lame compared 2 hers

CECILY

Wha???

Gabs, u r being crazy

GABRIELLE

Ok

CECILY

Ur life is super

U r going on a trip

CECILY

We have the pool 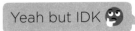 & Jennie's
pizza 🍕 🍕 🍕

GABRIELLE

Yeah but IDK 🤨

CECILY

Chill, Gabs 💆 💆

Maybe don't look @ the album so much ✋

GABRIELLE

Ok 👌

But I like to look @ it 🤨

CECILY

Yeah but not all the time 📱

Dear Journal,

I just lied to Gabby and I don't know why. She was saying how this one girl's life seems perfect on the camping album and I made it seem like I didn't know what she was talking about but I totally did and I feel the same way. I just felt really awkward admitting it for some reason. I don't know. Like it's not a good quality to be jealous and I couldn't say it out loud. But I am jealous. Everyone is going on a cool vacation at the end of the summer except for us. Prianka is going to India and Gabs is going to Texas with her dad, and this new girl Ivy who Gabby is kind of obsessed with is going to Maine with her whole family to this fancy resort. I never want to admit that I feel these things but I do.

Love, Cecily

HEARTS 4 days ♥ ♥ ♥ ♥ ♡ ❣ ♥

GABRIELE

R u seeing all these hearts on the photos
❣ ❣ ❣

It's craziness ♥

> **PRIANKA**
>
> I thought u wanted 2 be screen-free

GABRIELLE

Ha that lasted 2 min 😂 😂

No more 4 me

This album is really fun ♥ ♡ ♥ 💞

R u reading the comments ⁉️ ⌨️

> **PRIANKA**
>
> No I haven't checked it again

GABRIELLE

Cece ‼️

PRIANKA

I think she's still screen-free 📵 📵 📵

Can we discuss @ the pool 🩴 🩴

Getting ready 2 go 👙 👙 👙

GABRIELLE

K c u there 😎 😎

Cece, meet us if u see these texts 📲 📴 📱 📵

I'll call ur landline now ☎️ ☎️ ☎️ 📞 ☎️ 📞 ☎️

Ooh btw Ivy texted me 📲 📲

I was so excited 👏 👏

Prianka, Victoria

P V

PRIANKA

heading over 2 the pool

VICTORIA

K same 🚶

Ready for Best Summer Ever 2.0 💯 💯 💯 💯

PRIANKA

U seem to be the only 1 who really cares tho 😡 😡 😡

Life feels crazy, like everything is changing 24/7 😖 😵

And that really scares me 😬 😣 😦 😦

VICTORIA

Noooo we r all going 2 have fun

K love u & ur positive vibes, Vic

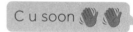

C u soon

VICTORIA

Vishal, Prianka

VISHAL

U home

PRIANKA

Yup ✔ ✔

VISHAL

U r never going 2 believe this

???

VISHAL

My cousin Akshara moved into that bldg in Mumbai with the pools on every balcony

PRIANKA

NO WAY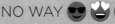

VISHAL

Yes I just found out

We r staying w her fam

PRIANKA

Omgggg so jealllllll

VISHAL

I knew u would be

PRIANKA

Ew rude

VISHAL

But u can come hang there

It's not far from ur fam right

PRIANKA

IDK will ask my mom later

VISHAL

Akshara is fab

U will like her

PRIANKA

K going 2 pool now

What r u up to

VISHAL

Playing video games

Arjun and Jared r coming over later

PRIANKA

Cool 😎

Come to the pool if u r bored

VISHAL

K

I'm the first one at the pool
All by myself on this lounge chair
Ready to start Best Summer Ever 2.0
I made that up
But it sounds good
Still feel bummed that I didn't like camping
My parents paid all that money
And I didn't have fun
The people were just so intense
Always so peppy about everything
And into deep thoughts
I don't think I'm like that
Everything feels spinny crazy scary
Changing all the time
TBH, IDK what's next
I guess I'll just write poetry
Until I figure it out

Prianka, Victoria

PRIANKA

Sorry to text behind their backs but do u c how they r like obsessed with the camping thing and the online album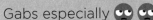

Gabs especially

VICTORIA

Umm

PRIANKA

She has not stopped talking about it

VICTORIA

I feel weird texting about them when they r right here

PRIANKA

True I get it. Text me tonight.

Yorkville Pool Lunch Menu

Mozzarella sticks
$5.95

Cheeseburger
$6.95

Hamburger
$5.95

Tuna melt
$7.95

Side of fries
$2.00

Hot dog
$2.95

Grilled chicken salad
$8.95

Fruit smoothie
$5.00

Scoop of ice cream
$2.00

Ice cream sundae
$5.00

Ice pop
$1.50

Can of soda
$1.00

Bottle of water
$1.00

Hi, guys—let's do this while waiting for our food. We did it at creative writing camp in Philly. It was so fun. I write one or two sentences then pass to Pri, she writes, passes to Cece, she writes, then passes to Gabs, and again and again until our food comes. Fun? Okay, I'm starting . . .

There once was a dog who was actually part human. His owners didn't realize it right away but eventually they did. His name was Barkin and he didn't like to do any actual dog things. He liked fancy people things. His favorite food was sushi. His favorite activity was lounging by the pool. But there was one problem. He was kind of lonely. His owners were rarely home. And he couldn't relate to other dogs. . . .

TRY OUT FOR THE YORKVILLE SWIM TEAM

Summer may only be three months, but did you know you can swim with your Yorkville buddies all year long?

It's true! You can!

Try out for the Yorkville Kids' Swim Team!

Stop by and see Sally Wembly in the pool office for more details.

Happy swimming!

Mama Anderson, Prianka

MAMA ANDERSON

Prianka, please tell Cecily she left her phone at home and it's buzzing nonstop

PRIANKA

Haha k

Mom, Prianka

MOM

Prianka darling, please put away your laundry when you return from the pool

PRIANKA

Ok

MOM

I do not want to have to remind you again

PRIANKA

OKAY

Prianka, Victoria

PRIANKA

Hi, Vic, u there

VICTORIA

Yeah hey 😎 😍

PRIANKA

Did it feel weird 2 be back in philly

I never even got 2 ask u

VICTORIA

Haha not really, it was an amazing time

I creative writing camp & was so good to be back with Nic & Kim

PRIANKA

Fab

VICTORIA

Guess u CAN go home again

PRIANKA

Huh **??**

VICTORIA

NVM

R u excited for

PRIANKA

Kinda

Nervous to be around family all the time & be on best behavior

PRIANKA

U know how family always comment on how much u've grown & stuff 🙄 🙄 🙄

VICTORIA

LOL yeah 😭 🙄

PRIANKA

But I think it'll be more fun than past years bc I know more peeps now like Vishal, Arjun and stuff 👩🏽 😳 😳 👩🏽 👨🏾

VICTORIA

So jeal 🙄 😨 🖤

Going to miss Arjie so much 😕 😕 😕

PRIANKA

Have u been seeing him a ton

VICTORIA

Kinda sorta IDK 🤷 🤷

PRIANKA

Oh

So can we pls discuss my BFFs

Haha umm

Kind of awk but ok

What do u want 2 discuss

I feel so awk w/ them

Like camping was ok but not the best 4 me

And now I feel so left out since I didn't love it

& one kid started a group text and it's like nonstop hearting and thumbs up and texts 24/7

Yeah

Sooooo

What do u think

VICTORIA

IDK I feel like it'll calm down 🕊️ 🕊️ 🕊️

I mean u all just got home 🏠 🏚️ 🏠

PRIANKA

Yeah true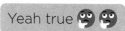

Wahhhh IDK 🧕 🧕

VICTORIA

I hear u 🙁 🙁

I felt that way when I moved here 🏯 🏯

Remember, LOL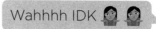

PRIANKA

Ha yeah sorry

VICTORIA

It's ok 👍👍

U can vent anytime 🗣️🗣️🗣️

I wonder why I am feeling
so frustrated with my friends
Waiting for Best Summer Ever 2.0 to start
I think it may
be because
it sorta
feels
like they
moved on
without me
I want it to be
like the old days

Just the 3 of us + Victoria
I want us to be
the only friends
we need
We're not exclusive
We just like each other best

From: Douglas Katz
To: Gabrielle Katz
Subject: Our trip

Hi, Gabs,

Welcome home from camping! I can't wait to hear all about it. Sounds like you had a great time and weren't homesick like you thought you would be. I'm so proud of you for trying this and I'm thrilled that you loved it.

Now onto our trip. . . . We're going to have so much fun! The hotel where we're staying has a pool on the roof! Woo hoo! Mom says you are considering joining the Yorkville swim team with your friends. So now you can practice. And I know you love room service, so we can definitely order a few times.

Ethan and his kids are so excited to see you. Remember them from when you were little? Eric is your age and Phil is one year younger.

Don't forget to pack bathing suits and goggles and good walking shoes and then whatever else you want to wear.

Love, Dad

Unknown, Gabrielle

MAYBE: ELI

Hi, Gabby?

I just realized I had your # from the roster

GABRIELLE

Hi

How r u

ELI

Good u

GABRIELLE

Good went 2 the pool today

ELI

Haha I know

GABRIELLE

Huh

76

ELI

I saw the photos u posted on group album

GABRIELLE

Oh right LOL

ELI

Looks like a cool place

So cool that u r still diving 🏊‍♂️🐬

GABRIELLE

It is 🏊‍♂️🏊‍♂️🐬

I'm going on a trip to Austin with my dad
soon 🎒👜🧳🌵

ELI

Cool

GABRIELLE

What r u doing the rest of the summer

ELI

Just hanging out

My grandparents r coming 2 visit from Israel

GABRIELLE

Oh awesome 😎😎😎

ELI

Have u ever been

GABRIELLE

No

I want 2 go 🇮🇱🇮🇱🇮🇱🇮🇱

ELI

U should def go 1 day

Best place ever

Amazing falafel obv 🧆🧆🧆

GABRIELLE

R u Israeli ? 🇮🇱🇮🇱🇮🇱🇮🇱

ELI

Yeah both my parents were born there

GABRIELLE

So  !!!!!!!!

ELI

I kinda wish we were having a Darren sing-along now LOL

GABRIELLE

Haha same same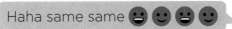

I wish we were dunking our cookies

ELI

Ha

Was so gross @ first but then good

GABRIELLE

I agree

I didn't expect to miss the group so much

79

GABRIELLE

Just not the same w/o u guys

ELI

Aw I know

GABRIELLE

I gtg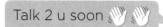

Talk 2 u soon

ELI

Ok bye

Gabrielle, Cecily

G C

GABRIELLE

Cece, r u still awake or even looking @ screens LOL

CECILY

Hi yes I decided 2 look @ my phone once a day @ night so I can keep up with camping album & group text but too much to catch up on 😱 😵 😱 😵 😎 😳

GABRIELLE

Haha I know ✔️

Eli texted me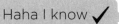

CECILY

Oooh 😵 😱

GABRIELLE

Did u know he's Israeli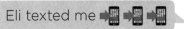

CECILY

No I barely talked 2 him 😕 😵

GABRIELLE

Haha me neither 😂 🤣 😂

I am only texting u bc Pri still seems annoyed about camping stuff 👧 👧

CECILY

IK but  side chats

Remember 🧐😡😠☹️

GABRIELLE

Haha yeah but it's awk 😒

Is this really a side chat 😕🧐

CECILY

Yes 🐶🐶

We can talk @ pool 2 morrow 👙👙👙🛁

GABRIELLE

Ok

CECILY

Mara comes home this weekend 😍😍😍

GABRIELLE

Oh cool 😎😎

Right when I leave LOL

CECILY

Well I'll have some1 to hang with 😊👯👯

GABRIELLE

Do u feel weird about seeing her 👯

CECILY

Not really

We wrote some letters 📩💌📮📝

GABRIELLE

COOL COOL

Do u still like her like her 😍

CECILY

IDK I think so 🌹❤️👩‍❤️‍👩

GABRIELLE

ok COOL

83

CECILY

K going 2 check camping album 1 more time & then go 2 bed 😴 💤 🛏️

GABRIELLE

Same 😴 😴

CECILY

Omg, Gabs, u have so many comments on the photo from the pool 💬 💬 💬 💬 💬

GABRIELLE

I feel bad its just u & me and not Pri but she didn't want 2 be in it 👭 👭

CECILY

IK

GABRIELLE

I feel so lonely w/o everyone 😿 😿

CECILY

Aw, Gabs 😭 😭

GABRIELLE

U @ least have Ingrid 👯 👯

CECILY

Yeah I'm so lucky when she tries to read my journal 😩 😩 😩

GABRIELLE

Still, 4 real, I'm all alone w/ my mom and then soon my dad & his weird friend

Gahhhhhh 💔 💔 💔

CECILY

U don't want 2 go on vacay w/ ur dad ⁉️⁉️

GABRIELLE

Not really no 😭 😭

Just dads, 2 boys & me = sooooooo awk 😫 😐 😐

CECILY

Oh no 😭 😵

Will think of fun stuff we can do b4 u go & Pri leaves 4 India

K luv u

Going 2 read comments 💬 💬 💬 💬 💬

CECILY

Same bye 💔 💔 💔

Cecily Anderson

Summer Essay

My dad always says the only constant in life is change. I think it's really true. Even physical changes are inevitable. My favorite jeans from last summer don't fit anymore. It's as simple as that. But there are also less superficial changes, of course.

We're all getting older and we're meeting new friends. We may find ourselves getting closer to new people than we currently feel to our old friends. In new and unexpected ways, too.

It's hard to say how exactly I've changed. I just know that I have.

SILVER GIRLS POOL DAY

 P V G C

PRIANKA

Pool @ 10?

VICTORIA

GABRIELLE

Yup

📞📞 Cece since she's still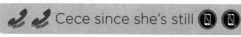

Although she comments on camping album so IDK 😨 😨

GABRIELLE

She's doing once a day phone check ✔️

PRIANKA

Oh ok ✔️✔️

VICTORIA

Impressive 😲 💯

I am every 2 min 😫 😫 😫

& I don't even know what u r talking about when u say camping album ⛺ ⛺ 🌅

GABRIELLE

Ha I'll explain ⛺ ⛺

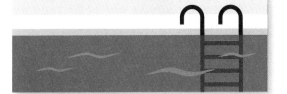

MAKE A SPLASH!

Who: Gabs, Pri, Cece & Vic

What: POOL DAY EXTRAVAGANZA

When: TODAY

Where: The Yorkville Pool (duh!)

Why: BECAUSE THIS IS BEST
SUMMER EVER 2.0

BEST SUMMER EVER 2.0 PARTY @ THE POOL DAY WOO

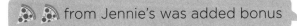

P V G C

PRIANKA

U guys, that was a truly fab day 🎉🎉🎉

🍕🍕 from Jennie's was added bonus

Who knew we could get food delivered 2 the pool ?

CECILY

I did LOL 😂😂😂

Breaking screen-free to be w/ u guys rn
👯👯😷😷

PRIANKA

Yay I am all cozy in pjs in bed & feel so clean from after pool shower

GABRIELLE

Me 2 😊 💗

Today was so fab, guys 🖤🖤🖤🖤🖤🖤

Was amaze 2 be 2gether & the balloons u tied 2 our lounges were so cute, Cece 🎈🎈🎈

CECILY

Glad u all enjoyed 👯👯😷 😷

VICTORIA

Hiiiii sorrrryyyy 🖐️🖐️🖐️

Was in the shower 🚿

Def a fab day ✴️🎆🎉🧜‍♀️

Can we do it again again pls ⁉️❓⁉️

CECILY

Yes but snack bar food k ❓

PRIANKA

K 🎉🎉

GABRIELLE

Woo 🎉🎉🎉

CECILY

Smooches 💋💋😍

91

Gabrielle Katz
Summer Writing Assignment

One major way that I've changed is that I feel a stronger sense of needing people around. When I was a kid, I really only needed my mom and dad. And then when I got older, my friends. But now it seems that I need big groups of people. Like maybe I'd be happy living on a kibbutz like they do in Israel. Then I'd always have people around.

I don't know why I feel so lonely all of a sudden, but I do.

This is getting very emo. Will probably revise.

Mom, Prianka

MOM

Prianka, darling. Hope you are enjoying the day at the pool. Your 7th grade schedule just arrived. I want to discuss it with you in case we need to make a change. Please come home after you finish swimming. Love, Mom

PRIANKA

Ok

MOM

NAME: Prianka Basak
Grade: 7th
Homeroom teacher: Ms. Lincoln

1st period 8:15 — 8:55
Homeroom — Ms. Lincoln — Room 63A

2nd period 9:00 — 9:40
English — Mrs. Kanel — Room 53

3rd period 9:45 — 10:25
Math — Mr. Kemp — Room 67

4th period — 10:30 — 11:10
Study Hall — Ms. Echley — Room 55C

5th period — 11:15 — 11:55
Lunch — Cafeteria

MOM

6th period — 12:00 — 12:40
Science — Ms. York — Room 72A

7th period — 12:45 — 1:25
Science Lab — Ms. York — Room 72B

8th period — 1:30 — 2:10
Elective period

9th period — 2:15 — 2:55
Social Studies — Mr. Marits — Library annex

32

Comments

♥ **Eli:** that hike was crazy

♡ **Ivy:** I know, thought I was going to pass out

♥ **Brianna:** I pretty much did pass out LOL

♡ **Ivy:** LOL, Brianna

♡ **Bex:** where is Cece rn

♡ **Leigh:** IDK

♡ **Jake:** she usually comments

♡ **Leigh:** we might need to get lives & not spend all day chatting on this album

♡ **Bex:** haha

♥ **Bex:** but since my parents don't allow social media this is a way to get around that LOL

♡ **Jake:** true

♥ **Prianka:** Cece is at the pool with me

♡ **Ivy:** tell her to sign on

♡ **Prianka:** she's anti phones during the day since the screen-free trip LOL

♡ **Jake:** oh

♡ **Bex:** ha!

♡ **Jake:** check out this butt

♡ **Bex:** ewwwwwwwww

♡ **Dimah:** OMG what

♡ **Prianka:** OMG no thank u, Jake

♡ **Jake:** LOL it's an arm butt

♡ **Jake:** not a real butt LOL LOL

♡ **Dimah:** still ewwww

♡ **Jake:** calm down

Mom, Gabrielle

MOM

Gabs, your schedule came for 7th grade. I know you've been waiting for it. Here's a pic in the meantime

```
YORKVILLE MIDDLE SCHOOL
STUDENT SCHEDULE

NAME: Gabrielle Katz
Grade: 7th
Homeroom teacher: Ms. Lincoln

1st period 8:15 — 8:55
Homeroom — Ms. Lincoln — Room 63A
```

MOM

2nd period 9:00 — 9:40
Social Studies — Mr. Tulipo — Room 64

3rd period 9:45 — 10:25
Math — Mr. Kemp — Room 67

4th period — 10:30 — 11:10
Study Hall — Mr. Arannsky — Room 55B

5th period — 11:15 — 11:55
Lunch — Cafeteria

6th period — 12:00 — 12:40
Science — Ms. York — Room 72A

7th period — 12:45 — 1:25
Science Lab — Ms. York — Room 72B

8th period — 1:30 — 2:10
Elective period

9th period — 2:15 — 2:55
English — Mrs. Ecarem — Room 76B

SILVER GIRLS 2GETHER 7th GRADE?!?!

GABRIELLE

See pic 4 my schedule

Here's mine 2

So glad we can text these so we can all 👁 👁 👁 👁 together

Omg, Gabs, we have almost all classes 2gether

GABRIELLE

Hmmm is this a good thing or a bad thing? 😉 😉 😉

LOL

VICTORIA

Took my mom 7 decades 2 figure out how 2 send it 😠 😠 but here is the top of my sched

VICTORIA

```
YORKVILLE MIDDLE SCHOOL
STUDENT SCHEDULE

NAME: Victoria Melford
Grade: 7th
Homeroom teacher: Mr. Tulipo

1st period 8:15 — 8:55
Homeroom — Mr. Tulipo — Room 64

2nd period 9:00 — 9:40
Study Hall — Ms. Framingham — Room 83a

3rd period 9:45 — 10:25
Math — Mr. Kemp — Room 67

4th period — 10:30 — 11:10
English   Mr. Goldwell   Room 66A
```

VICTORIA

Bottom is cut off

Ugh will send rest later

PRIANKA

Cece, what about ur schedule ❓❓

GABRIELLE

Her is @ home

Wahh we will just have to wait &

VICTORIA

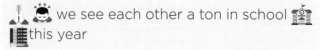 we see each other a ton in school 🏫
🏢this year

So far we all have math together 💯 💯

From: Prianka Basak
To: Akshara Mehta
Subject: BOMBAY TRIP

Dear Akshara

I am sooo excited to meet you. Vishal and Arjun have only said the nicest things. And your apartment building looks so amazing! Do a lot of kids live there? How insane to have a pool on every terrace! I am freaking out thinking about it. Can't wait to hang out.

XO Prianka

From: Akshara Mehta
To: Prianka Basak, Vishal Gobin, Arjun Gobin
Subject: RE: BOMBAY TRIP!!!

Hi, guys—

So excited that you're all coming to India. Prianka, I added you to this email because I hear you're friendly with my cousins Vishal and Arjun. We're going to have the best time. I have tons of plans in store. Get ready to play cricket against real players. JK—it's simulated cricket but will be SO much fun. And so many restaurants for you to try.

Cant wait to meet you, Prianka!

xoxo Akshara

Mama Anderson, Prianka

MAMA ANDERSON

Prianka, so sorry to bother you. Can you please ask Cecily if she wants   for dinner? I think we are going to grill. You are welcome to join. Please let me know. Thank you. Love, Elizabeth

PRIANKA

Ok

Prianka, Victoria

PRIANKA

Vic can u show this 2 Cece?

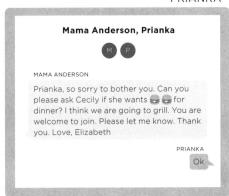

I'm talking 2 sally about the swim team & don't want 2 forget.

Cece never has her phone grrrr 😠😠😠😠😠😠

VICTORIA

Ok np

Mama Anderson, Prianka

MAMA ANDERSON

Cecily, are things okay between you and Prianka?

You know I am always here if you want to talk

PRIANKA

Haha this is Prianka

MAMA ANDERSON

Oops meant to send that to Cecily to see when she does her nightly phone check. So sorry!

PRIANKA

It's ok

SILVER GIRLS SWIMMING TOGETHER FOREVER 👙

VICTORIA

So we r all doing the swim team 🏊👙🏊
🏊🌊👙

PRIANKA

Yes 🏊🏊🏊🏊🏊🏊

VICTORIA

Cece, I think this is during ur phone time
LOL 📱➡️📴📴📱🤳

GABRIELLE

LOL yes 📴📴

And yes 2 swim team 👙🏊

PRIANKA

Will u have ur phones with u so I don't have
2 take all messages from moms 😠😤😠

CECILY

OMG, PRI

R u ok

So harsh

PRIANKA

I'm fine

GABRIELLE

R u sure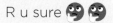

U seem pretty stressed since we've been back 💆💆💆

PRIANKA

I'M FINE 🔥🔥🔥🔥

GABRIELLE

Don't yell @ us

PRIANKA

Ugh can we go back to discussing swimming 🦇🏊

CECILY

Sure ✓

Btw my schedule didn't come

GABRIELLE

Prob 2morrow

CECILY

Also I will tell my mom to stop texting u
messages 4 me ✓

PRIANKA

Ugh stop, Cece

I gtg

C u guys 2morrow

Hopefully less drama

Night z^z z^z z^z

Gabrielle, Cecily

Srsly what is her deal

CECILY

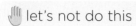 let's not do this

GABRIELLE

I am worried tho

CECILY

Discuss in person

CECILY

Night 🛏 🛏

Eli, Gabrielle

ELI

I'm about to upload my pics from the trip

I have such a funny one of you doing that zip line swing

So happy they let us have regular cameras on the trip

GABRIELLE

Omg

Why did u take that

I was freaking out 😳 😳 😳 😳 😳 😳

ELI

Haha it's ok

It's a good pic

ELI

I'm going to post it

Is that ok

GABRIELLE

Um sure

ELI

Did u ever see the note I wrote u

GABRIELLE

I did 😳 😳

ELI

Ok

GABRIELLE

It was really nice 😎 😊 😊

ELI

Tjank u

Gabrielle, Cecily

GABRIELLE

Cece, r u there **???**

Eli took a pic of me that day on zip line swing & he is going to post it 😮 😳 🤫

CECILY

Hi I'm here 💁

GABRIELLE

Isn't that weird 🤖 👾 👽 🤡

CECILY

IDK people took a lot of pics 📷 📷 📷 📷 📷 📷

He's posting all his pics right 💁‍♂️ 💁‍♂️

GABRIELLE

Yeah I guess so 🙍

CECILY

So it's

GABRIELLE

I don't think I like him

I like Colin more

CECILY

Don't worry

Just go with the flow

GABRIELLE

I guess

CECILY

I wish my schedule would come

GABRIELLE

It will soon just chill

Victoria Melford
Summer Writing Assignment

There is no doubt that I have changed tremendously since last summer. I didn't even live in Yorkville last summer. I was still in Philly then and I switched schools mid-year. It was brutal. But I survived it. I am stronger now. I am tougher now. I am more outgoing. I am more patient. I am not as easily frustrated. I am not as desperate for friends. I think I am a better version of myself now.

Change is good. No doubt about it.

Tarzan Gabby Katz

Comments

♡ **Jaylen:** hahahahaha #crushedit

♥ **Simmie:** best swing ever

♥ **Gabby:** hahahah I didn't know this photo was being taken

♡ **Jake:** #elistalker

♡ **Eli:** #amnot

♡ **Cecily:** #sofunny

♥ **Dimah:** #missuguys4ever

- ♡ **Ivy:** #gabsisthebest
- ♥ **Jaylen:** #wercoolestgroupever
- ♡ **Eli:** #inthehistoryofoutdoorexplorers
- ♡ **Brianna:** #woo
- ♥ **Dimah:** #howmanydaysuntilnextyearstrip

Mom, Prianka

MOM

Prianka darling, are you awake? Ignoring me? I've knocked on your door three times and I am concerned. Love, Mom

PRIANKA

I'm up

Be downstairs soon

MOM

Do you want eggs?

PRIANKA

No

Thank u

MOM

Have you finished packing for India?

PRIANKA

I started but not done yet

MOM

OK. Please let me know if you need help.

PRIANKA

K

MOM

I am getting the hang of this texting.

PRIANKA

Ok but stop ✋✋✋

Please

Soon I will be in India
The land of my people
Connected with family
And friends
Old and new
Challenges and dreams await me
I want to finish this summer
And say it was great
I don't want to be disappointed
Maybe I stress too much
Maybe not every experience
can be fabulous
But maybe it can
Maybe it is
all
in
our
control

Dear Cecily,

How are you? How's being
home from camping? I can't wait
to hear all about it.

Do you like this stationery? My grandma
just sent it in a package for me.

Camp is going great. We went on this
overnight to Boston and this is so weird but
we all slept on the floor of this synagogue.
I mean, with sleeping bags and stuff. But it
was actually really fun.

We went on a boat tour of the
city. And we saw a comedy
show. And we all went

out for this big pasta dinner.
Such an amazing break
from camp food! Camp food is
disgusting by the way. Did you like
the food on the camping trip? Did you
have to cook it yourself? So many questions.

This girl in my bunk, Pearl (isn't that a
cool name?), had her first kiss at the
temple in Boston and now it's all she can
talk about it. And who has a first kiss at
a temple? So funny, right? But also, it's
like, enough already. But I guess it's a
big deal. It was with this kid
Alex. He's been coming to
camp forever. I don't know

if they're going out now or what. But I guess Pearl will fill us in. She's new this year and everyone thinks she's so cool. She lives in Brooklyn and goes to some super artsy school where they don't even have grades and they just write and paint all day. It actually sounds cool. Imagine life without math? Well, you're good at math. So I guess that wouldn't appeal to you.

Anyway, this letter is really long. Thanks for writing to me. Write back soon.

xo Mara

Dear Mara,

I'm writing you back right away so I don't forget. Not that I would forget. But you know what I mean. I'm leaving for the pool in a few minutes. I've been going every day since we've been back. I'm excited for you to come home and we can walk to the pool together. Also did I tell you I might try out for the swim team with Pri, Gabs, and Victoria? I can't remember if I wrote you that or not. After you suggested it, I thought it would be really fun.

Anyway, Pearl is a cool name. I guess she's having a fun summer at camp even though it's her first time. Why does everyone think she's so cool? Just because of the Brooklyn thing? Are you friends with her?

How are your other friends? I forget their names. One is named James, right? I always remember that because it's such a cool, unique name for a girl, I think.

Do you ever wonder if you'd be a different person if you had a different name? Maybe Cecily isn't the best name for me. Would I be different if my name was James? Would you be different if your name was Pearl? Is it strange that I think about these things?

Pri is being so weird since we've been home. It's like she hates Gabs and me because we had fun on the trip. I don't know. People are adding photos and stuff to our group album and it's kind of like our own version of social media. But you know how my mom won't allow that... I don't think she knows this exists. And anyway it's just people from the trip. Although Victoria wants to join.

This is getting to be so long, too. And probably not so interesting.

Off to the pool. Write back soon.

Love you lots, Cecily

To: Cecily Anderson, Prianka Basak, Gabrielle Katz, Victoria Melford
From: Sally Wembly
Subject: Swim Team

Hi, girls—

Thank you for your interest in the Yorkville swim team.

I'm leaving these notes for you at the pool welcome desk because I am not sure if I will see you today and I wanted to update you on the swim team situation. It looks like we will start practice at the end of August. We'll have meets against other neighborhood pools: Fieldston Lake, Barnham Hill, Waverly Heights, and Clover Creek. I think it'll be a great season.

During the year, we will have practice two or three afternoons a week starting at 3:30 p.m.—most likely Tuesday, Wednesday, and Thursday, so please make sure that fits your schedule.

Please feel free to spread the word to any other Yorkville kids that like to swim and may want to join the team.

See you soon,
Coach Sally

From: Prianka Basak
To: Akshara Mehta
Subject: PACKING

Hi, Akshara,

Is it weird to email you again even though I don't know you? I hope not. But I sort of feel like I know you already.

I just wanted some help with packing. I'm bringing jeans and tees and skirts and dresses and bathing suits and sandals and sneakers. I know it's hot there.

Am I missing anything specific? Do I need anything fancy? My mom says no but I don't always believe her. LOL.

Thanks for your help!
XO Prianka

Hey, Cecily!

I'm writing you twice in one day but I forgot something! I've been thinking that we should do that backyard camping thing when I get home. Remember we talked about it but we never ended up doing it because it rained? Well, when I get home I will be super sad missing camp, and it sounds like you are too right now, so can we please do it? My family has tents, but I think yours does too. So either way.

See you soon!
xo Mara

Unknown, Prianka

MAYBE: AKSHARA

Hi, Prianka 👋🏽 👋🏽 👋🏽

Vishal gave me your #

PRIANKA

Hiiiii 👋🏽 👋🏽 👋🏽

Now u r in my

AKSHARA

YAY 🎉 💃🏽 🎉

So excited to hang so soon

PRIANKA

Me too 👏🏽 👏🏽 👏🏽 👏🏽

AKSHARA

Check ur email re: packing 📖 📖

AKSHARA

& I sent u websites 4 my fave restaurants

Come HUNGRYYYYYYYY 😊 😋 😊

PRIANKA

K thx 🙏 🙏

From: Outdoor Explorers Staff
To: Outdoor Explorers Group
Subject: Online photo album

Helllooooo, Explorers!

We hope you're all settling into home life okay. We're thrilled that you're enjoying the online photo album. Just a reminder to keep it civil and kind and respectful. You can upload pictures to keep everyone posted on your life at home, but it must be APPROPRIATE, aka Outdoor Explorers appropriate.

Keep exploring!
George and the other counselors

"Wherever you go . . . go with all your heart."—Confucius

POOL DAY!!!!

P · V · G · C

PRIANKA

Good morning, friends

My last pool day b4 India so let's make this count

C u there LOL

Cece, where r u

VICTORIA

She is still 💤 💤 💤 in the morn

PRIANKA

Oh duh

Where is Gabs

GABRIELLE

Hi sorry 🖐 🖐 🖐

PRIANKA

Let's do that story thing again, k

VICTORIA

K

Colin, Gabrielle

C   G

COLIN

Gabs when do u leave for ur trip

GABRIELLE

In a few days

COLIN

Do u want 2 hang out b4 u go

GABRIELLE

Yeah maybe

COLIN

Sorry I haven't been @ pool

GABRIELLE

Yeah, Pri leaves 2morrow so we have been @ pool every day 🏊🏊🏊

COLIN

K

I want 2 show u this thing I have been painting

GABRIELLE

Ooh cool 🎉🧜🎉🧜

So Barkin lived his life in a very fancy way. He ate sushi and lounged by the pool and got his hair done at a fancy dog salon. Some days he would high-five himself in the mirror for how awesome his life was. Other days he would cry his eyes out. He saw what other dogs were doing (he used a computer) and felt that they had way more friends than he did. So even though his life was fancier, it was so much more lonely. He came up with a plan. . . .

My friends don't understand me anymore
I am about to go all the way across the world
and they don't even care
And what if I feel out of place there, too?
I don't want relatives to comment
on how much I've grown
If you know what I mean
It's so awkward
What if I feel
out of place
everywhere?
I don't know where
I feel in place
Is there such a thing as in place?

Ivy, Gabrielle

IVY

Hey, Gabs

GABRIELLE

Heyyyyyyy I miss u soooooooo mucccchhhhhhh 😟😢😫😩😩

IVY

Me 2 🦉🦉

U are my fave new friend

GABRIELLE

Ha thanks same 2 u 🐿️🐿️

IVY

What's up 🐵🐵

GABRIELLE

Um not much 💃🏻👟👧🏻👟

@ the pool now 🦈🏊🏻🏊🏻🤿👙

IVY

Oh tell Pri & Cece I say hi 👋👋👋

GABRIELLE

K we r eating lunch 🌭🍔🍕

Here's a pic of Pri's turkey wrap 🦃🦃🌯🌯🌯

IVY

LOL 😂😂😂

What's up with Eli & Colin 👦👦👦

Helllooooo ⁉️⁉️

Where did u go 😫😵😫😵😫😵

IVY

I'm going 2 Maine on vacay with my whole fam l8r

Bad cell reception there

May not be able 2 text or post 2 album

Gtg smooches

OUTDOOR EXPLORERS 4 LIFE

IVY

Guys, what happened 2 our group txt

JAKE

IDK

JAKE

People ran out of stuff to say LOL

JAYLEN

And no one wants to see any more arm
butts, Jake. LOL

DIMAH

Everyone is just chatting on the album now

CLARA

True 🎈🎉

IVY

I was just texting Gabs & she disappeared
😮😮😮

DEFINITELY NOT BEST SUMMER EVER 2.0

PRIANKA

U guys, I am so furious with u

Gabs, how could you send Ivy a pic of my food

Sooo embarrassing

And then Cece—u just laughed about it

None of u even get how I feel

Except Vic

Helllooooo

Why r u all ignoring me

NM be BFF with the outdoor explorers

I don't need u anymore

Guys, since neither of you responded to my text when I stormed away at the pool and walked home all by myself and none of you even followed me, I'm passing the shared notebook around. I'm really upset about how things are going. I'm leaving for India and I feel like things are super weird between us. You don't even care. All you care about is the stupid online album and the stupid trip and when I tell you I feel left out and hurt, you don't even care. And how could you send that photo, Gabs? You didn't even ask permission. It's gross to send a pic of someone's food. Eating is personal! And then Ivy laughed and you guys did too. Victoria is the only nice one! We had that one fun pool day and that was it for Best Summer Ever 2.0? Come on, guys. I feel like you don't even care about me anymore since I didn't like the camping trip. Have you moved on to bigger and better things without me? Do you even care that I'm leaving for India so soon? I'm going across the world. It's a big deal.

Okay, bye. Love, Pri

Pri, I am so glad you said something. I feel like things have been off since we got home. You never really open up to us about how you're feeling. I mean we know you didn't like the trip but what else? Is there more than that going on? I'm sorry about the picture. It wasn't nice. I thought it was just funny but I didn't realize it would hurt your feelings. You are super sensitive lately. Do you know that? Why are you so super sensitive? Do you have any idea? Okay, walking over to Cece's house to pass this along.

I really don't want us to all separate on bad terms.
I'm sorry you're feeling so left out, Pri. We love
you, obviously. But we cannot control if you have
the best summer ever. Maybe some summers aren't
as good. I shouldn't have laughed at the picture
Gabs sent. Are you worried about going all the way
to India? Do you feel like you will miss stuff here?
We will miss you but don't stress. It will be great.
Your family loves you, and you won't be camping. So
there!

Also, my schedule didn't come! I don't know why.
My mom is calling the school tomorrow. Walking
over to Pri's house now to put shared notebook
through the mail slot. My mom is walking me over
because it's dark. Ha!

I am nervous about India because I don't know all these relatives and what if they're creepy? Also, you guys will continue to have more fun without me and I'll feel even more distant when I get back. Then we'll keep growing more and more and more distant and who knows if we'll even be CPG4eva when I get back. We obviously like different stuff. Maybe we're totally growing apart.

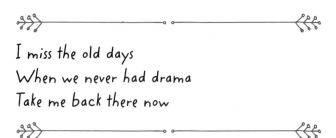

I miss the old days
When we never had drama
Take me back there now

Vishal, Prianka

VISHAL

Yo r u on the way 2 the airport

PRIANKA

Yup

VISHAL

Did u know u, me & Arj are all on same
flight

PRIANKA

Ha just found out

PRIANKA

Victoria will be sooo jealous

VISHAL

Haha

Arj will really miss her

PRIANKA

IK they r in love

VISHAL

Ha

PRIANKA

I am so happy to get away from my crazy friends

VISHAL

Really

U luv ur friends

PRIANKA

Yeah but since camping they r wack

VISHAL

Oh

See u soon

Victoria, Prianka

VICTORIA

Have u seen Arjun yet

PRIANKA

I am still in the car on the way to the airport

VICTORIA

Will u text me when u see him

PRIANKA

Yes but chill, Vic

VICTORIA

Ok

Tell him I miss him

& that he is the best boy in the world

PRIANKA

LOL tuxedo boy ok

CPG4EVA 4 REAL

C P G V

PRIANKA

Guys, I can't believe u showed up @ the airport

GABRIELLE

CECILY

Couldn't let u go 2 India w/ things all awk

PRIANKA

Well thx

CECILY

You needed a hug and a good send-off so you can relax & just have fun there & know we love you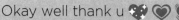

PRIANKA

Okay well thank u

OMG Cece u r on ur phone & it's not ur usual time

CECILY

Just for a few min 😛 😛

PRIANKA

Miss u guys already 😰 🐱

Will be so hard 2 stay in touch in India w/ time diff and Wi-Fi 📳 🔕 📱 📶 📲 ➡️📱

My mom did not get overseas data package

Since I snuck phone on camping trip she reallllly wants me 2 unplug LOL

I downloaded app that works well there I think & can connect to my contacts just in case 📱📱

But Mama Basak will prob take 📱📱 away 🙏 🙏 🙏 🙏

Maybe I can message u from a laptop ⌨️ ⌨️ 💻 💻

GABRIELLE

It'll be ok, Pri ✔️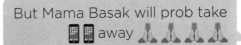

PRIANKA

U have 2 keep me updated with schedules, Cece

CECILY

I will

CECILY

My mom called the office 5 times

PRIANKA

Gabs at least I have u & Vic 2 get me thru math 👏👏

I hear Mr. Kemp is a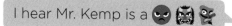

GABRIELLE

Woo 🎐🎐🎈🎉🧜🐰🐰

Did I tell u I am going 2 Colin's 2 see his painting 🖼️🖌️👨🎨

His parents set up this old shed to be an art studio for him in the backyard 🌳🌲🌳🌳

CECILY

So cool 🖌️👨🎨

PRIANKA

Interesting

PRIANKA

Why is Colin like a 75 year old man tho

GABRIELLE

Pri

PRIANKA

JK

I gtg

We r about 2 go thru security

GABRIELLE

Ily

CECILY

WE LOVE U, PRI

Not Delivered

Victoria, Prianka

VICTORIA

Did u talk to Cece & Gabs @ the airport

My mom wouldn't let me go bc my aunt was coming over 😣 😓

But things r not awk b/t us so I figured it's
`OK`

PRIANKA

Yeah

VICTORIA

U r always so good @ saying what's on ur mind 👏 👏 👏

PRIANKA

IK

VICTORIA

Maybe time away will be good

PRIANKA

Maybe 🫥

So glad u & I have science & history & lunch 2gether & we have gotten closer this summer 🎀🎉👧

VICTORIA

Me 2 🖤🤍🖤🤍

PRIANKA

I gtg 💌💕✈️

VICTORIA

Bye 🖤

Boredom on this flight
Missing my friends
Family asleep
Does this even count as poetry?
Calming to write this way
Dreaming of sleep
Feeling alone
Empty water bottles all around me
Darkness outside
What is the meaning of anything?
Do I even know who I am?

From: Edward Carransey
To: Cecily Anderson, Elizabeth Anderson
Subject: Cecily's schedule

Hello!

Hope you're both having a lovely summer. It appears there was a glitch with Cecily's schedule and somehow the computer put her into the eighth grade! That's what caused the holdup and it took us a while to figure out what happened. We should have it for you shortly. Many apologies for the delay.

Best wishes,
Mr. Carransey

You must be the change you want to see in the world.
—Gandhi

From: Cecily Anderson
To: Gabrielle Katz, Prianka Basak, Victoria Melford
Subject: HI

Hi, guys!

I'm emailing you because I don't know Pri's Wi-Fi situation and I don't want to send texts that end up costing the Basaks tons of $$. My schedule got messed up because somehow they put me into 8th grade by mistake. LOL.

I really hope I have it soon. I'm super nervous I won't get the pottery or astronomy electives I wanted and my schedule will be terrible. And what if we don't have lunch together? How will I survive?

Prianka, how was the flight? I think you've been there for a day and you haven't written us yet!

Love, Cece

Eli, Gabrielle

ELI

Gabby, I am coming to your area in a few weeks

My cousins live kind of close to you

GABRIELLE

Who are ur cousins

ELI

Sam, Nessa, and Shir Navell

GABRIELLE

Oh haha

IDK them

ELI

Would u want 2 hang out

GABRIELLE

Maybe

GABRIELLE

Text me b4 and I'll see if I'm free

ELI

K cool

Have fun in Texas

Ivy, Gabrielle

IVY

Ummmmm I am sure u know this already

... But Eli reallllllllly likes u

GABRIELLE

Haha IK

But how do u know

IVY

Hahaha I just do ‼️

Do u like him ❓❓❓

GABRIELLE

IDK

IVY

He's cute I think 👨🏻

GABRIELLE

Yeah but I think we r better as friends 👨‍👩‍👦‍👦

I like Colin 👱 👱 👱

IVY

Ok well figured I'd tell u

GABRIELLE

Thanks 👍

IVY

GTG 🖤 🖤

IVY

We just got back from Maine & I'm going to NYC 4 a Broadway show w my mom 🍎🗽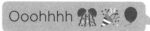

GABRIELLE

Ooohhhh 🎆🎇🎈

So fab 🎉🎉🎉🎉

IVY

Haha yeah 👯 👯

I'll post pics 🤳📱📱

I may meet up with Marley and Leigh when I'm there 🖤🖤🖤

GABRIELLE

Oh

So jeallllllll 😼

Victoria, Prianka

VICTORIA

Pri, r u there 🙄🙄🙄

How is Arjie 😎😎

I've texted him 💯 times and 0️⃣0️⃣ response

Hellooooooo 😭😭😭

Feels like u guys r on another planet 🌍🌏🌎🌐

Soooooo far away 😿😿😿

HELLO FROM INDIA

PRIANKA

Guyssssss, I am messaging u on laptop while rents r asleep

We r 9 hours and 30 min ahead of you guys

Have been screen-free during the day and kind of 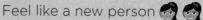 it

Feel like a new person

But wanted 2 do a quick check-in

GABRIELLE

Hahaha u haven't missed much

Well u have missed some stuff on the camp album but u can catch up

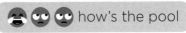 how's the pool

GABRIELLE

Fun as always 😹😿

PRIANKA

I miss u guys soooooo much 😿😿

GABRIELLE

We miss u 2 😿😿

VICTORIA

How is Arjun 🧑🏾

I have texted him 3000000 times 😾😿
🙀😾😾

+ nada response 🙄🙄

4 real 😾😾

PRIANKA

 He doesn't have Wi-Fi @ his cousin's place 📶

163

It's broken or something

Plus his mom is trying to limit 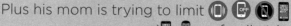   on family trip

VICTORIA

Nooooooo

PRIANKA

So what have u guys been up to

VICTORIA

Not much

Just regular stuff

Pool etc

GABRIELLE

I went 2 Colin's 2 hang

PRIANKA

Did u kiss in his art shed LOL

GABRIELLE

CECILY

Hi

Have been avoiding phone but when I saw it was u, Pri, I had to check in

I miss u soooooooooo much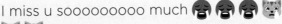

I had no idea Gabs went 2 Colin's

VICTORIA

Me neither

GABRIELLE

His little art shed is so cool

I think his parents r really trying 2 encourage it

CECILY

That's so cool

GABRIELLE

I go to Texas 2morrow 🤠 🤠

Kinda freaking out 😱 😶

PRIANKA

Y **??**

GABRIELLE

Just feel awk with my dad's BFF & his kids
😬 😬 😬

Plus will miss pool time & need to fig out
stuff with Colin & IDK just not feeling the
trip 🤠 🤠 ★

CECILY

It will be great, Gabs, 4 real 👍 👍

U didn't want 2 go camping either & look
how that turned out 🌠 🌠

GABRIELLE

Ha true IDK

Cece, did ur new schedule come yet

CECILY

Nooooooooo

Oh wahhhhh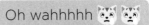

If u don't hear from me 4 a while know why

VICTORIA

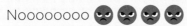

CECILY

GABRIELLE

From: Gabrielle Katz
To: Prianka Basak
Subject: FREAKING OUT

Hi, Pri,

You're the only one I can talk to about this because you know how it feels. I am freaking out about this trip with my dad. I don't know these kids and TBH my dad and I aren't that close anymore. I am going to be the only girl. 2 dads, 2 boys & me. What am I going to do? HELP ME. Why are you so far away when I need you?

Xoxo, Gabs

From: Edward Carransey
To: Cecily Anderson, Elizabeth Anderson
Subject: Schedule update

Hello!

I didn't want to keep you waiting any longer so I am attaching a copy of Cecily's schedule. A hard copy will come in the mail as well.

Enjoy the rest of summer!
Edward Carransey

You must be the change you want to see in the world.
—Gandhi

YORKVILLE MIDDLE SCHOOL
STUDENT SCHEDULE

NAME: Cecily Anderson
Grade: 7th
Homeroom teacher: Ms. Lincoln

1st period 8:15 — 8:55
Homeroom — Ms. Lincoln — Room 63A

2nd period 9:00 — 9:40
Honors Math — Ms. King — Room 64

3rd period 9:45 — 10:25
Social Studies — Mr. Libson — Room 67

4th period — 10:30 — 11:10
Honors Science — Mrs. Ecrof — Room 55B

5th period — 11:15 — 11:55
Science Lab — Mrs. Ecrof — Room 55B

6th period — 12:00 — 12:40
Lunch — Cafeteria

7th period — 12:45 — 1:25
Honors English — Mr. Wallace — Room 70

8th period — 1:30 — 2:10
Elective period

9th period — 2:15 — 2:55
Study Hall — Mr. Mintz — Room 55

WE DON'T HAVE LUNCH TOGETHER OMG HELP ME NOW WHAT IS GOING ON OMG

CECILY

Omg u guys 😠😠😧😦😵😐😲😬

I am the only one of all of us in the 6th period lunch 😠😠😠😠😠

I didn't even know all 7th graders didn't eat together 🌭🍔🍕🥪🥪🌮🥙🍴🍽️

Where r u guys ⁉️❓⁉️❓

I am breaking my no-screen-vibe rule rn 🙀🙀

Ahhhhhhh

WE DON'T HAVE LUNCH TOGETHER OMG HELP ME NOW WHAT IS GOING ON OMG

VICTORIA

So sorry I was @ a tutor 📚 📖 📚

Did I tell u my mom forced me 2 get a math tutor ✖️➕➖➕👩🏽

She wants me to move into honors math & maybe whole honors block 😫 😵 😫 😵 😫 😵

GABRIELLE

Sorry was packing 🧳 🧳 👜 🎒 👝

OMG, Vic, that is crazy 😲 😦 😳 & we wont have math 2gether

Cece, u have a diff lunch bc of ur honors classes I think 👩🏽 🏫 😳

GABRIELLE

They had 2 split 7th grade up this yr bc all the new kids who r coming since West Lake Middle is under renovation 👷👷‍♀️⚠️🏗️

CECILY

How do u know all this 😂🤣😂😿

GABRIELLE

My mom told me 👧👧

Haha remember she's on the school board 😹😹

CECILY

Oh yeah LOL 😫🤣

Not fair honors kids have 2 be split up tho 😧😵😖😩😫😣😤😠😡

GABRIELLE

Def not 🙅‍♀️🙅‍♀️

CECILY

I am fuming mad 😣😩😖😤😡😡

GABRIELLE

Sorry none of us r in honors unless Vic switches 😟😟😟😟

VICTORIA

😟😠 U should say something, Cece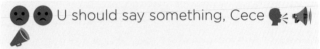

CECILY

I might write a letter 🙇‍♀️🙇‍♀️🙇‍♀️

GABRIELLE

Good luck 🍀🕉️🤞👆🎱

Back 2 packing 👜🎒

BTW that photo of my suitcases open and all my tank tops has gotten 23 hearts so far 🖤🖤🖤🤍🤍

CECILY

Omg 😵😵😵

From: Cecily Anderson
To: Prianka Basak
Subject: I need your help

Dear Pri,

I know you're screen-free during the day in India so I wanted to email you instead of text. I'm so worried about Gabs. She's become obsessed with Ivy and comparing her life to hers and she thinks Ivy's so perfect. It's really sad. And all she cares about is how many people heart her online pics. Do you have any advice?

I love you, Cece

I'm not afraid of storms, for I'm learning how to sail my ship.—Louisa May Alcott

WE DON'T HAVE LUNCH TOGETHER OMG HELP ME NOW WHAT IS GOING ON OMG

PRIANKA

U guys

I am way behind on email so sorry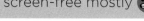

& u sent me all those texts @ 3am + u know I am screen-free mostly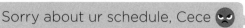

Sorry about ur schedule, Cece

Now it's middle of   4 u guys so u won't answer

Grrrrr time diffs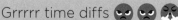

I give up

Back to bliss

Cecily, you must come out of your room so we can discuss this. Locking yourself away because you have a different lunch from your friends doesn't make sense. Please come down and let us talk through this rationally. Love, Mom

Mom, Cecily

CECILY

Stop leaving me notes

U don't get it

Cecily, this is silly. Come downstairs and let's talk.

No, it's not

Gabrielle, Cecily

Cece, guess what? We're not going to Texas!

We're going to Block Island!

Remember when I went all the time when we were little? And we took the ferry and stayed at that cottage right on the beach?

GABRIELLE

Texas was fake out which woulda been cool

OMG Block Island is my fave place on the planet

My dad surprised me !!!!!!!!

CECILY

GABRIELLE

R u ok

CECILY

😠😠

😠😠😠😠😠😠😠😠😠

Don't want 2 talk

GABRIELLE

● ● ●

Gabrielle, Victoria

GABRIELLE

Vic, r u there ⁉️❓⁉️❓

VICTORIA

I'm always here LOL

Tnx 4 the log-in 4 the camping album

Weird but kind of u 2 share

Mega interesting

Def want 2 go next year

GABRIELLE

Ok but I need 2 talk 2 u about something

Stressed about Cece

VICTORIA

What is it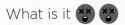

GABRIELLE

She's super mad about the lunch thing & doesn't want 2 talk 🗣💬💭

Can u try 2 help 🤞🙌🙏

I feel so bad Pri & I r away 😥😞😔

VICTORIA

IDK will try ✌️✌️✌️

GABRIELLE

K thanx 🙌

Getting on ferry bye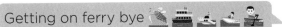

From: Prianka Basak
To: Gabrielle Katz
Subject: RE: FREAKING OUT

Dear Gabs,

Don't worry. I'm sure it will be okay. You always end up loving everything. Think about camping and how you were dreading that and then thought it was so great. I'm always here for you. Love, Pri

From: Prianka Basak
To: Cecily Anderson
Subject: RE: I need your help

Dear Cece,

I sensed that before I left. I think it's an issue. She is too concerned with other people and what they're doing and what they think of her. That's why she needs to keep track of all the hearts on the album. I'm glad you reached out. We can help her.

I love you, Prianka

I feel like I am
a better friend
From far away
India has allowed
me to be
my best self
Calmer
More caring
Truly helpful
Sometimes distance
is
the
answer

Dear Journal,

I am so mad about this schedule thing. I am separated
from all of my friends. It makes no sense to divide
the lunch periods based on honors track and regular
track. It's elitist actually and so rude. It is unjust! I
cannot stand this. I am going to fix this and change the
system!

Love, Cecily

Mara Kramer
Summer essay assignment

Thinking back to last summer, I barely even recognize myself. I was so isolated and introverted. I only spoke to the same two friends.

I feel that I've opened up and grown. I feel more comfortable in my skin. I feel like I can take risks and expand my horizons.

I feel more free. I feel like the best is yet to come.

From: Cecily Anderson
To: Prianka Basak
Subject: Epiphany

Dear Pri,

I am not admitting this to Gabs, but I think I care too much about the hearts on the album, too. I am so upset barely anyone liked my hammock picture. Am I cool in real life? I don't feel cool in this online computer world. Is that even a thing? I don't even know when you will see this email. :(

Love, Cece

I'm not afraid of storms, for I'm learning how to sail my ship.—Louisa May Alcott

Victoria, Cecily

VICTORIA

Hi, Cece 👋 👋

VICTORIA

R u ok ❓❓

CECILY

No not really 😣 😣

VICTORIA

What's wrong ❓❓

CECILY

So 😖😠😤😫😣😖😣😟😔😞🙇 about schedule

Also I posted a pic of the hammock in my backyard and only 2 people liked it 😔 🙁

VICTORIA

Umm 😵 😵

CECILY

I made it look super artsy &

VICTORIA

VICTORIA

Maybe not everyone likes hammocks

CECILY

IDK

VICTORIA

Lmk if I can help

I can come over

CECILY

K thanks

Intervention?

GABBY

Check out my view, guys. . . . On the way to Block Island! Woo! #ferryride

IVY

OMG so beautiful 💯 👆 🙌

BRIANNA

#jealous

CLARA

#jealousx2

DIMAH

#jealousx1000000000000

ELI

Have so much fun

JAKE

I love Block Island!

CECILY

Miss u, Gabs. 😍😘💜

Victoria, Cecily

VICTORIA

I   🕵️ what u mean

Gabs got a ton of comments 💬🗨️💥

CECILY

??

On the camping trip album

LOL u r on it now too 🙄 🙄

Ha Gabs gave me the log-in ✅ ☑ ✔

I want 2 go on the trip next yr

Ok ✔

I gtg 💁

Emailing principal C. 📥 📧

From: Mom
To: Cecily Anderson
Subject: Re: FW: Schedules for next year

Looks good, Cece-baby. Proud of you. Love, Mom

> **From:** Cecily Anderson
> **To:** Mom
> **Subject:** FW: Schedules for next year
>
> Mom, is this email okay? Let me know. Love, Cecily

I'm not afraid of storms, for I'm learning how to sail my ship.—Louisa May Alcott

>> **From:** Cecily Anderson
>> **To:** Principal Carransey
>> **Subject:** schedules for next year
>>
>> Dear Mr. Carransey,
>>
>> I hope you're enjoying your summer. I wanted to write to you about the 7th grade schedules. I don't think

it's fair for all the kids in the honors classes to have a different lunch than the kids in the regular classes. I know we have many more kids this year because of the renovation of West Lake Middle School. But I think there is a better way to split us up. This system will only make the kids in regular classes feel bad and the kids in honors feel bad, too. I don't mean to be disrespectful, but it seems like an elitist system. Dividing everyone up this way.

I am happy to come in and meet with you in person so we can discuss this.

Thank you,
Cecily Anderson

I'm not afraid of storms, for I'm learning how to sail my ship.—Louisa May Alcott

MISS MY GIRLS

GABRIELLE

Did u see how popular my ferry pic was

Where are my girls

GABRIELLE

Where is everyone

VICTORIA

Hi

CECILY

Pri is hardcore it seems

GABRIELLE

Yeah

Did u guys see I broke my record on 🖤 🖤 on album

CECILY

OMG, Pri was right u r obsessed with this album, Gabs 🥷 🙄 🙄

GABRIELLE

So r u

CECILY

U r more obsessed

GABRIELLE

Ugh

I gtg

From: Prianka Basak
To: Cecily Anderson, Gabrielle Katz, Victoria Melford
Subject: stuff

Hi, guys –

I have to tell you how amazing this screen-free life is. Cece, you were so right. But it's more than just not texting.

I'm sending you an article that my new friend Akshara sent me about how bad needing attention on social media can be. It takes us out of what we are doing in real life and hurts our self-esteem in the long run. We cannot evaluate our lives based on what others think and how they respond online.

I don't know why it took a trip across the world for me to realize how much I needed to unplug and how much we all need to step away from that album.

Please read the article.

I'm going to do this cricket simulation thing now where we go to a place and it feels like we are playing cricket with real players, like the famous professional ones. It's like a giant video game but like with real people. Cricket is a big deal here. Should be fun. Will tell you all about it when I am home.

Love, Pri

Here's the article link!!

Mara, Cecily

M   C

MARA

Hiiiiiii

Remember me

I'm hooomeeeee

Omg ‼️💗❗‼️💗❗

I didn't realize it was 2day ❗❗❗❗

MARA

Yeah!

CECILY

Victoria & I are @ the pool 🏊🏊🏊

Want 2 come ⁉️⁉️

MARA

Well I just got home but maybe another day

CECILY

K talk later 👋

I am now screen-free
During the day
Feels silly to write about this
But I feel great
Like a thousand bricks are off my shoulders
I don't think of checking my phone
I actually notice what's around me
I am listening better
And paying attention
Sharing personal stories with new friends
Akshara feels like a soulmate BFF
My great-uncle Kamal has taught me so much
About life
And my heritage
Screen-free = clear mind
Screen-free = happier Pri
Who knew?
Maybe Mama Basak was right
I will never tell her that though
No

From: Edward Carransey
To: Cecily Anderson
Subject: RE: schedules for next year

Dear Cecily,

Thank you for voicing your concerns. As you know, coordinating the schedules for five hundred Yorkville Middle School students is a complicated puzzle.

I would be happy to discuss this with you (and your parents if you'd like) in person. Please call the main office and set up an appointment.

All my best,
Mr. C

*Sent from my handheld device. Please excuse any typos.

LONGEST GROUP TEXT IN THE HISTORY OF TEXTING

GABRIELLE

U think we can keep this text going until next summer's trip 🗣️ 🗣️ COOL 👍

IVY

LOL maybe 👍 👍 👍

BRIANNA

I hope so 🙌 🙏 🙇 ✌️

JAKE

#yeswecan

CLARA

#def

DIMAH

#yesssssssssss

GABRIELLE

We are the Outdoor Explorers and we are here to say . . . 🎵🎵🎶

IVY

Ahhahahahahahahahahaahahahah

BRIANNA

LOL LOL 😂🤣😂😁

JAYLEN

4 sure

Prianka has left this chat

Cecily, Gabrielle

GABRIELLE

Cece, did u see the pic Ivy posted at that resort 😮😫😮😫😵

  How insane is that pool 💯💯💯

And the one with all her cousins together jumping in the air

Yeah 👍 👍

So amazing right

I wish I had tons of cousins

Yeah but Gabs ✋ ✋ u r on Block Island rn
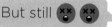

Ur life is fab 💯 👍

But still

TBH I think this stuff has made u crazy 😵

CECILY

I hate 2 agree w Pri & that article but I think she's right 😲 😵 😵

GABRIELLE

Wdym

CECILY

That article she sent 🤭

When u see all these pics it starts 2 make u crazy 🙄 💁

And u r comparing urself 2 others too much ✋ ✋

& ur life is great too 😍 😍

GABRIELLE

IDK I like seeing the pics 🙄

CECILY

But still

Think about how it affects u

CECILY

I am telling u this bc it started 2 affect me 2 & TBH I got jealous 🙄❤️😳❤️😳

GABRIELLE

When

CECILY

A little bit ago w/ all of Ivy's fancy amaze pics 🙁🙁😠😠

GABRIELLE

Why didn't u tell me 😳🙁😳

CECILY

IDK I was embarrassed 😠😊😔😔😞

GABRIELLE

Well thank u for sharing now 💔

I gtg ✌️💁

CECILY

Love u 💔🖤💔

Mara, Cecily

MARA

Sooooo excited 4 sleepover

CECILY

Me tooooooooo

My mom is going 2 get amazing snacks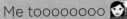

MARA

Yummmmmmmmmm

Mom, Cecily

MOM

Cecily, what snacks would you like for the Mara sleepover? I am at the grocery store.

CECILY

Cookies, chips, iced tea, sour straws, pretzels, cucumbers, lemonade, carrots, hummus, s'mores stuff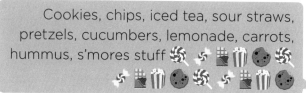

MOM

Wow. Ok.

CECILY

Thank u 🙌

India feels like another world
It is another world
We are shielded from poverty here
We live far away from it
We are shielded from poverty at home
We live far away from it
We are so fortunate & we don't even realize
Do we close our eyes on purpose?
Do others close them for us?
What if I were born someone else?
And someone else was born me?

COMING HOME FROM INDIA EARLY

PRIANKA

U guys, I have to break screen-free life to update u

I need 2 come home from India early

This is crazy

My dad's cousin from NJ fell and he has 2 have emergency surgery

& my dad is only one who can help

Anyone there

Helloooo

COMING HOME FROM INDIA EARLY

CECILY

Just saw ur texts

Super worried bc u didn't use emojis

So sorry

Is his cousin ok?

PRIANKA

IDK really

It's so messed up

My mom, bro, and I were gonna stay but it's too chaotic

CECILY

So when do u come home

PRIANKA

2 days

So sad to leave early

Was having so much fun

Really felt like myself here & so happy 2 hang w/ Akshara

CECILY

Sorry u r sad but we will all be 2gether again 🙌 (≡ 👌

VICTORIA

✴️ 🎆 🎇 🎉 🧜 👯

I'm going 2 plan a welcome back bbq 🌭 🌭 🌭

Maybe we can do Best Summer Ever 3.0 😵 😵 😵

What: WELCOME HOME EVERYONE BBQ

When: Saturday @ 4 p.m. (or whenever you show up)

Where: Victoria's house!

Who: US!

What to bring: Yourselves!

YOU'RE INVITED!

ORIGINAL CPG4EVA

CECILY

Guys, I took Vic off chat bc she doesn't know how I feel about Mara 🏃🏃

We are doing backyard camping tonight 🌳🌳🌳🌲🌲

OMG I am nervous but excited 😌😊😍

I should just tell Vic how I feel about Mara 🙄🙄🙄

IDK why it is a secret 😻😻

Where r u guysssss ❓❓❓

Mara, Cecily

MARA

On my way 2 backyard campout

CECILY

MARA

Ha u love emojis

CECILY

From: Victoria Melford
To: Cecily Anderson, Prianka Basak
Subject: RE: Intervention

Dear Cece and Pri,

We can do it @ the BBQ but then let's make sure it turns to fun stuff too. OK?

Xo, Victoria

> **From:** Cecily Anderson
> **To:** Prianka Basak, Victoria Melford
> **Subject:** RE: Intervention
>
> Dear Pri and Vic,
>
> Ummmmm. This feels intense. But I get what you mean.
>
> Love, Cece
>
> *I'm not afraid of storms, for I'm learning how to sail my ship.—Louisa May Alcott*

From: Prianka Basak
To: Cecily Anderson, Victoria Melford
Subject: Intervention

Dear Cecily and Victoria,

I am emailing this because I don't want to accidentally send a text to the wrong person. I think we need to have an intervention with Gabs. This album thing and the group texts with camping peeps have gotten out of control. She is becoming really psycho.

Akshara told me they did this with one of her friends when the girl started planning out her online posts days in advance. She started deciding what to do each day based on if it would make a good post or not. It was all she thought about.

We have to make sure that doesn't happen to Gabs.

Since I am coming home early, we can do it sooner.

What do you think? Maybe at the BBQ @ your house, Vic?

Love, Pri

Mom, Cecily

MOM

Cecily, you guys okay out there? Don't want to disturb but it is getting kind of chilly.

CECILY

Mom, we are FINE.

Thx

MOM

Ok. Please come in if you get cold. I am leaving the back door open. Dad and I are going to sleep now. I think Ingrid is still up. Love, Mom

CECILY

Ok pls stop texting

Thank u tho

MOM

Ingrid, Cecily

INGRID

Don't worry I am not spying on you

CECILY

Um?

INGRID

I can't even see the tent from my window

CECILY

Ok then why r u texting me this

INGRID

Just bc I feel like u think I'm spying

CECILY

I didn't

INGRID

Ok love u have fun

Victoria, Cecily

VICTORIA

 today?

CECILY

Yeah but later on

Just got up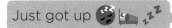

VICTORIA

U slept so late

CECILY

Mara slept over last night & we stayed up late

VICTORIA

Oh ok

Meet u there later by lounges, usual spot

Bring Mara too 👀 👀 👀 👀

From: Prianka Basak
To: Cecily Anderson, Gabrielle Katz
Subject: RE: OMG

I agree with Gabs about the sleepover. Please tell us more. I am about to get to the airport to leave India. Wah. I wasn't even that excited to come and now I am sad to leave. I loved being with family and surrounded by my culture. And the pools on every balcony in Akshara's building were beyond amazing! Wait till you see what fab stuff I'm bringing back!

But please tell us more stuff. It is a long time until I get home. And, Gabs, you gotta chill with the hearts. Whoa. Also, I stopped looking at the album weeks ago. Love, Pri

From: Gabrielle Katz
To: Cecily Anderson, Prianka Basak
Subject: RE: OMG

YOU CANNOT DO THAT, CECE. So unfair. Please tell us. Also, did you see I broke my record? 44 hearts on that pic of my flip-flops on the beach on Block Island. xo Gabs

> **From:** Cecily Anderson
> **To:** Gabrielle Katz, Prianka Basak
> **Subject:** OMG
>
> OMG you guys! Mara just left. We had the backyard campout. I have so much to tell you it is insane. But I think it should wait for in person. I have to update Vic. I feel bad she doesn't know about any of this.
>
> Love you lots, Cece
>
> *I'm not afraid of storms, for I'm learning how to sail my ship.—Louisa May Alcott*

CPG4EVA

CECILY

Moving this 2 text

I think my mom may snoop on my email more than phone IDK

I'll tell you 1 thing . . . . We kissed.

Not during the sleepover but the next day when I walked her home and her whole fam was in backyard we had quick kiss

She said not to tell anyone

But I don't think that included you guys 😳

Where r u guys now ? ? 😳

K bye

Cecily, Victoria

CECILY

I forgot I can't come to the pool 😞 😞

I have a meeting with Mr. C. to discuss schedules 🙏 👲 🙏 👲

I'll ttyl 👋 👋

VICTORIA

Sorry just saw these texts

Was

From: Edward Carransey
To: Yorkville Middle School Students; Yorkville Middle School Parents; Yorkville Middle School Faculty
Subject: Change in Schedules

Dear Yorkville Middle School Community,

It has come to our attention that there has been a glitch in the schedules for the upcoming school year. We will have to make some adjustments and will be sending the students a revised schedule as soon as time permits.

Please accept my sincere apologies. In my thirty-year career as principal, this has never happened.

Wishing you all a wonderful end to summer,

Edward Carransey

You must be the change you want to see in the world.
—Gandhi

HOME HOME HOME

P G C V

PRIANKA

U guys, I'm home

Just saw email about schedules

WIGO

GABRIELLE

Hiiiiii

U r not out of the loop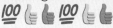

Cece got schedules changed

PRIANKA

OMG go Cece

VICTORIA

227

When r we all hanging out

GABRIELLE

Today @ pool?

CECILY

Hiiiiiii

Sorry was outside

I will be @ pool later but I gtg

Mara, Cecily

MARA

Hi

CECILY

Hi

MARA

The other night was so fun

I know I told u a million times but here is a million + 1

CECILY

LOL I agree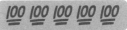

MARA

But pls promise u won't tell anyone about u know what

CECILY

💯 💯 💯 💯 💯

IDK why it is a big deal but ok

MARA

I am a private person

U know that

CECILY

IK 💔 ❤️ 💔

R U coming 2 the pool later?

My friends will all be there

MARA

Maybe IDK

May go back 2 school shopping with my mom

CECILY

Oh fun

MARA

I will ttyl tho

CECILY

k bye

MARA

Soooooooo......

PRIANKA

So r we on 4 intervention with Gabs @ V's bbq

CECILY

Um ok 😨 😨

PRIANKA

U think it's a bad idea 😨 😨

CECILY

TBH it seems to have kind of died down 👧 👧

PRIANKA

She just wrote the thing about the hearts on the flip-flops pic 😨 😨 😠 😠 🚫 🚫 📵 📵 📵 🙈 🙈 🙈

CECILY

Oh right

CECILY

And she does compare herself 2 Ivy a ton

PRIANKA

See

U were obsessed too but u calmed down

CECILY

LOL thanks

That article u sent really made a diff

PRIANKA

Thanks

VICTORIA

Let's do it right away @ my bbq and then
fun

232

CECILY

PRIANKA

WHERE ARE MY CAMPING PEEPS

GABRIELLE

Guys, where is everyone

I miss u all sooooooooooo much

IVY

Hiiiii

ELI

Yo Yo

JAYLEN

Hey

GABRIELLE

Back from BI . . . At my other happy place

Dear Gabs,

You may wonder why we are sitting in a circle in Victoria's backyard and classical music is playing and I am writing in a brand-new shared notebook (Victoria is now a part of it!) while you sit right in front of us. But the truth is, we are worried about you. You have become obsessed with getting attention—mostly on the camping album. It's like you need everyone to be focused on what you're doing and how amazing it is. And then you get upset and compare yourself to others. Do you see you are doing this? I don't want you to feel attacked. But we are concerned. And we love you. Passing to Cece now for her thoughts.

Hi, Gabs. You know I love you. And you know I loved the camping trip too. (Sorry, Pri.) But the thing is, now you are so consumed with it. You keep track of how many people like your photos or heart them or whatever and the group texts, too. I got kinda crazy, too, and then Pri pointed it out to me and I realized I needed to pull back. I feel so much better now. I don't check the album as much. I try not to obsess over what other people are doing. I was starting to get really jealous, too, so I get it.

Hiiii first of all. So happy to be in the new shared notebook. Gabs, even though I wasn't on the camping trip, I started to see how obsessed you got. Sometimes it was all you could talk about—not about the trip but the album and all the attention. And that's not you! You're fun and friendly and smart and outgoing and a great swimmer. There's more to life than showing off to people! We don't want to lose you to this craziness. And it wasn't making you happy, either! At all! You just compared yourself to others SO much. And you don't need to! You're great! You're Gabs!

OMG you guys. This is so weird. I snatched the notebook away because I had to weigh in. You really think I have gone crazy with this? I mean, I appreciate that you care but I am okay. For real. I will stop talking about it so much.

Also, so super awk to sit all silently in a circle while you're writing to me. TBH VERY AWK.

You don't have to stop talking about stuff. Just realize how it affects you. That's it. You're cool and fun and you don't need people "hearting" your pics to make you realize that.

I agree 100%.

Totally—we love you, Gabs! We had to call your attention to this. You didn't even realize you were doing it.

I will think about it. This is still super awk though. You guys realize that, right?

Haha. Sometimes things are awk. I mean, hello? We have had tons of awk stuff in our friendship. Bra shopping with the moms? Pooping outside that one day on the camping trip? (Will explain to you later, Vic.)

Ew. Can we not discuss that again?

Haha. Ok. You have a point. I am just glad we are all home and can get ready for school and rock 7th grade.

Same. I agree. Even though I was having fun in India, it's relaxing to be home before school starts. And we have a great year ahead—woo hoo electives!

Well, glad we got everything out in the open now. We can just enjoy my BBQ with no stress. . . . But I'm sure there's more drama coming down the pipeline.

LOL, Vic. That sounds so ominous. Dun Dun Dun . . . Let's have fun. I'm excited.

Hahaha. But Vic's kinda right. TBH, IDK what's next. But maybe that's the exciting part. . . .

GLOSSARY

2 to

2gether together

2morrow tomorrow

4 for

4eva forever

4get forget

any1 anyone

awk awkward

bc because

BFF best friends forever

BFFAE best friends forever and ever

BI Block Island

b-room bathroom

b/t between

c see

caf cafeteria

comm committee

COMO crying over missing out

comp computer

DEK don't even know

deets details

def definitely

diff different

disc discussion

emo emotional

every1 everyone

fab fabulous

fabolicious extra fabulous

fac faculty

fave favorite

Fla Florida

FOMO fear of missing out

fone phone

FYI for your information

gd god

gtg gotta go

gn good night

gnight good night

gr8 great

hw homework

ICB I can't believe

IDC I don't care

IDEK I don't even know

IDK I don't know

IHNC I have no clue

IK I know

ILY I love you

ILYSM I love you so much

JK just kidding

K OK

KIA know-it-all

L8r later

LMK let me know

lol laugh out loud

luv love

n e way anyway

NM nothing much

nvm never mind

nums numbers

obv obviously

obvi obviously

obvs obviously

OMG oh my God

ooc out of control

peeps people

perf perfect

pgs pages

plzzzz please

pos possibly

q question

r are / our

ridic ridiculous

rlly really

RN right now

sci science

sec second

sem semester

scheds schedules

shud should

some1 someone

SWAK sealed with a kiss

TBH to be honest

thx thanks

TMI too much information

tm tomorrow

tmrw tomorrow

tomrw tomorrow

tomw tomorrow

totes totally

ttyl talk to you later

u you

ur your

urself yourself

vv very, very

w/ with

wb write back

w/o without

WIGO what is going on

whatev whatever

wknd weekend

WTH what the heck

wud would

wut what

wuzzzz what's

Y why

ACKNOWLEDGMENTS

A zillion thanks to: all the readers, Dave, Aleah, Hazel, the Greenwalds, the Rosenbergs, the BWL Library & Tech Crew, Maria, Stephanie, Katherine, Aubrey, Vaishali, Ann, Erin, Molly, Emily, Liz, and the whole Katherine Tegen Books team! And especially Sonia and Nandita for all the India help.

LISA GREENWALD lives in NYC 🍎 w/ her husband & 2 young daughters 👨‍👩‍👧‍👧. She 💜s: 😎 📚 🏃‍♀️ & 🎬. Summer is her favorite season ☀️ 😎 🍉 🍨 🍦 🌅 👓. Visit her 💻 @ www.lisagreenwald.com.

Don't miss Lisa's next book: *13 & Counting*!

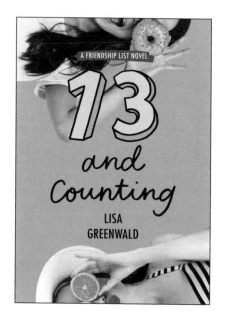

More great books by
LISA GREENWALD!

The Friendship List

TBH

KATHERINE TEGEN BOOKS
An Imprint of HarperCollins Publishers

www.harpercollinschildrens.com